PUFFIN BOOKS

The Little Explorer

Stanley, the little explorer, is determined to find the pinkafrillia, the rarest flower in the world. He sets off on his long voyage, and is joined by Knots, the sailor, and Peckish, the parrot. As they journey through the jungle of Allegria they have all sorts of exciting and sometimes dangerous adventures!

Margaret Joy was born on Tyneside. After graduating from Bristol University she became a teacher. She now lives in North Wales, where her husband is headmaster of a school for deaf children. She has contributed many stories to BBC TV's *Playschool* and BBC Radio's *Listen with Mother*, and has written a number of books for children, both fiction and non-fiction. She has four grown-up children.

Also by Margaret Joy

TALES FROM ALLOTMENT LANE SCHOOL
ALLOTMENT LANE SCHOOL AGAIN
HAIRY AND SLUG
HILD AT ALLOTMENT LANE SCHOOL
THE LITTLE LIGHTHOUSE KEEPER
SEE YOU AT THE MATCH

Margaret Joy

The Little
Explorer

Illustrated by Toni Goffe

PUFFIN BOOKS

For Marion, Gay and Mary

PUFFIN BOOKS

Published by the Penguin Group
27 Wrights Lane, London W8 5TZ, England
Viking Penguin Inc., 40 West 23rd Street, New York, New York 10010, USA
Penguin Books Australia Ltd, Ringwood, Victoria, Australia
Penguin Books Canada Ltd, 2801 John Street, Markham, Ontario, Canada L3R 1B4
Penguin Books (NZ) Ltd, 182–190 Wairau Road, Auckland 10, New Zealand

Penguin Books Ltd, Registered Offices: Harmondsworth, Middlesex, England

First published by Viking Kestrel 1989
Published in Puffin Books 1990
10 9 8 7 6 5 4 3 2 1

Printed and bound in Great Britain by
Cox and Wyman Ltd, Reading, Berks.
Filmset in Linotron 202 Times

Contents

1 Stanley Sets Out

Auntie Annie waved her hanky at the big ship.

"Goodbye, Stanley," she called. "Goodbyeee . . ."

The little explorer waved back. He felt quite sad to be leaving. But he'd been saving for years for his boat ticket – and now he was off.

"Look after our garden and greenhouse," he called.

"Of course," she cried, nodding.

"You never know," Stanley called, "I might just find the pinkafrillia."

"Wonderful!" she exclaimed. "Have you packed your hot-water bottle?"

"I won't need it," he replied.
"I shall be hot enough in the
jungle."

Knots, the sailor, undid the ropes, and the ship moved towards the open sea. Stanley waved until Auntie Annie's hanky was just a white speck. He still felt sad but he was excited too. He was sailing out to sea on a big ship to the island of Allegria. There he was going to do some exploring, and look

for the famous pinkafrillia
flower – the only one of its kind
in the world.

The ship chugged on through
the waves. Seagulls flew
overhead. Stanley watched the
sun go down until it was dark.

The stars seemed to be winking at him and saying, "Don't worry, Stanley, you'll be all right."

"I hope so," he thought, "I hope so."

Then he went down to his cabin and fell fast asleep in his bunk.

2 Two's Company

The ship chugged on for six days and six nights. Every morning Stanley studied his map of Allegria, and then went up on deck. He looked from east to west and north to south, but there was only sea all around. When he woke up on the seventh day, the sun was shining in through the porthole.

In the distance he could see land and tall trees. He dressed quickly and went up on deck. He blinked in the bright sunlight.

"Phew, it's going to be warm in the jungle," he said.

"Going exploring, are you?" asked Knots, the sailor.

Stanley nodded. "I've always wanted to explore," he said, "and now I'm going to search for the famous pinkafrillia."

"Pinkafrillia?" repeated Knots.

"Yes," replied Stanley. "It's the rarest flower in the world. There's only one left, and it's growing on top of the Cliffs of Pickapetal on the other side of the island of Allegria."

"I've always fancied being an explorer, too," said Knots. "I've had enough of being a sailor. Like some company?"

Stanley looked at him.

"You look strong and sensible," he answered. "Right, Knots – we'll explore together."

Soon the ship sailed into Allegria harbour and was tied up. The captain said goodbye to Stanley and Knots.

"We'll be back here on the first day of next month," said the captain. "If you're not here, we'll sail without you."

"Right," said Stanley.

He pulled his rucksack on to his back. Knots slung his kitbag over his shoulder. They waved to the captain and crew, then set off.

3 First Day in the Jungle

The jungle was hot and steamy. Drops of water dripped from all the trees. The leaves made a roof over the jungle and hanging from the branches were loops of thick creepers. All

around there were bushes
covered in flowers with
wonderful perfumes. Butterflies
fluttered by, tiny humming-
birds darted to and fro and
insects scuttled about.

Stanley and Knots looked
round with wide eyes; there was
so much to see.

"Wow," said Stanley.

"What a place," said Knots.

"And what a noise," said
Stanley.

20

The jungle echoed with the
sounds of animals and birds. In
the distance was the roar of a
mighty river.

"Wow," said Knots again. "What a place."

They made their way through the jungle, staring at all the new and wonderful sights. Suddenly a screech rang out from a nearby tree. The little explorer pushed his way through the

undergrowth. A beautiful red and green parrot had got her wing caught in a branch; she was stuck. She flapped her other wing about but she couldn't pull herself loose.

"Free-ee me-ee," she screeched. "Free-ee me-ee, plee-ase!"

Stanley tugged and tugged at
the branch and at last the parrot
managed to pull her wing free.
She shook her ruffled feathers
and hopped on to Stanley's
shoulder.

"See-ee – I'm free-ee," she squawked happily.

She began to look for food, pecking about on Stanley's shoulder and on his jungle helmet, tap-tap-tap.

"I think she's peckish," said the little explorer. "Let's stop and have a bite to eat with her."

"Aye, aye, cap'n," said Knots.

They sat on a log and shared
their bread and cheese.

"Here you are, Peckish," said
the little explorer to the parrot.
"Some for you, too."

Stanley brought out a bottle
of Auntie Annie's beetroot

wine. He drank a little, then Knots took a swig too. Peckish put her beak down into the bottle and swallowed a few drops.

"Whee-eee!" she screeched in surprise.

By now it was getting dark. Stanley and Knots decided to set up camp for the night.

"The ground looks a bit
damp," said Stanley.

"No problem," said Knots,
"I'll make two hammocks."

He reached up and pulled
down a few hanging creepers.

He wove some other creepers in
and out of them. Then he tied a
few strong knots (he was good
at that) and the hammocks were
soon ready. He looped them
over strong branches so they
each swung between two trees.

"There," he said, "we'll rock
to sleep like babies."

They zipped themselves into
their sleeping-bags and lay
down in the hammocks. Peckish
perched near their heads and
snapped up any insects that flew
too near.

Knots dreamt that he was in
his bunk in the ship. Stanley
dreamt of a beautiful flower like
a pink bell.

In the dark sky far above the
stars seemed to be winking at
one another, and the moon
shone down on the roof of the
jungle.

4 To the Rescue

Next morning they rolled up their sleeping-bags and packed them away. They washed in a pool of water caught in a large leaf. Peckish showed them some fruit that they picked and ate for breakfast.

"Time we got going," said the little explorer. "It's still a long way to the Cliffs of Pickapetal."

"Aye, aye, cap'n," said Knots.

"Today," said Stanley, looking at his map, "today we've got to get to the White River."

Peckish led the way, flying ahead of them. Suddenly she saw something behind a bush. At first it looked like the sun shining on speckled leaves. But then Peckish saw that it was a big cat with black spots on her golden fur – a leopard. She screeched at her but the leopard didn't move.

She was lying on her side, licking her paw. She looked up

at Peckish with her bright golden eyes. Then she held up her paw. Peckish saw that a long thorn was stuck deep down between the pads.

Peckish squawked and flew back to Stanley and Knots. They followed her and found the big cat lying there.

"Poor thing," said the little explorer. He opened his rucksack and took out his first-aid kit. "Good thing I packed the tweezers," he said.

He squeezed the tweezers
until they nipped hold of the
thorn. He pulled the thorn
slowly out of the leopard's paw.

The big cat swished her long tail and blinked at him with her bright golden eyes. Then she rubbed her head against his leg to say thank you and padded away into the bushes.

They set off again.

"Phew," said Knots, mopping his face. "It's never as hot as this at sea."

They marched on. Ahead of them was a wide patch of very green moss. It looked smooth and soft. Stanley and Knots stepped on to it and heard a loud sque-e-lchhh . . . They began to sink into the soft mud hidden under the moss.

"He-e-lpp!" shouted the little explorer. The mud was up to his knees, and he couldn't pull his feet out.

"Mayday, mayday," shouted Knots, as sailors do when they're in trouble at sea. The mud was up to his knees, too,

and his feet were still sinking.
Peckish screeched and
squawked as loudly as she
could. The noise rang through
the jungle.

Suddenly a flash of black and gold leapt out from the bushes. It was the leopard. She let her long tail fall across the marsh in front of Stanley and Knots. They grabbed hold of it and clung on tight. The mud was now nearly up to the tops of their legs.

The leopard began to pull. She pulled and pulled. Her shoulders took the strain. Stanley and Knots held on tight.

"Nee-early, nee-early!" screeched Peckish.

The leopard gave a last mighty pull. There was a loud sucking sque-e-LCHH! as Stanley and Knots shot out of the mud.

"Like corks from a bottle," gasped the little explorer.

The leopard blinked at them and padded away. She was glad she'd been able to help.

5 A Raft on the Rapids

Stanley looked at the map.

"We're a long way from where the pinkafrillia grows," he said, "and we've still got to cross the White River. Let's go."

"Aye, aye, cap'n," said Knots.

They pushed through the bushes. There was a loud roaring noise. Suddenly there in front of them was the White River. They stared in dismay.

"Oh!" cried the little explorer.

"My eye," said Knots.

Now they knew why it was called the White River. As far as they could see, upstream and downstream, was white water.

It was racing round rocks,
rumbling and roaring, splashing
and swirling, sucking and
seething, frothing and foaming.

"How are we going to cross
that?" said Knots.

"We could ride on a raft,"
said Stanley. "We could race
down the rapids on a raft."

"A raft? Don't be daft," said Knots.

"Why not?" cried the little explorer. "I'm not going back to Auntie Annie's yet. I've got to get to the Cliffs of Pickapetal and see the only pinkafrillia in the world. So we *must* cross this river. Come on, show me how to make a raft."

Knots shrugged. But he
swung his kitbag off his shoulder
and set to work. First they
found four thick branches that
had fallen down, and they
pulled them to the river bank.

Then they laid two of the
branches across the other two,
sideways. (If you want to see

how they did it, lay the first two fingers of one hand across the first two fingers of your other hand.)

Next Stanley pulled creepers round the branches, and Knots tied them in place with the tightest knots he could make. He slung his kitbag back on his shoulder. Stanley put his rucksack on his back. Then they put the raft on the water and jumped on. They lay down on their tummies, and held on *very* tightly. The noise of the water was so loud it frightened Peckish. She stayed close to Stanley.

"Ready?" shouted Stanley.

"Aye, aye, cap'n," shouted Knots.

Peckish hated getting her feathers wet, so she clung to Stanley's helmet. The water

quickly pulled the raft away
from the bank. It shot out into
the white water and whirled and
swirled. Foam flew up into their
faces. They were soon wet with
spray. Peckish looked like a
bundle of wet feathers. But they
were all still holding on *very*
tightly.

The water was taking them downstream, bumping and bashing and splashing. But at the same time, they were moving slowly across to the other side. At last, with a whirl and a whoosh, the raft shot into a little bend by the other bank.

Stanley grabbed a branch and pulled the raft in to land. They jumped on to the bank and sat down to dry off in the sun.

Peckish flapped the water from her wings and flew off. She soon came back with a pineapple hanging from her beak. Knots took a packet of ship's biscuits from his kitbag. The little explorer opened a tin of corned beef, and they had a delicious supper.

That night Knots made two more hammocks, and the roar of the White River lulled them to sleep.

6 A Bridge Over the Abyss

They walked on for many more days through the jungle. Knots had blisters on both his heels.

"I'm good at running up and down steps," he said, "and climbing up and down ladders, but all this walking is wearing out my feet."

The little explorer got out his
first-aid kit.

"Good thing I brought a big
box of plasters," he said.

Suddenly one day, there in
front of them, was an enormous
crack in the ground. It was very,
very deep. Stanley looked at his
map.

"This is called Earthquake Abyss," he said. "There must have been an earthquake that made the ground crack open."

"How shall we cross it?" said Knots. "I hope you don't want us to jump," he gulped. He was looking down, down, at the bottom of the abyss, far below.

"Jump? You silly lump. We need a bridge."

They found a big branch and rolled it to the edge of the abyss. Then they stood it upright.

"He-eeave!" screeched Peckish.

"Ready?" said Stanley.

"Steady," said Knots, nodding.

"GO," said Stanley, and they both let go.

The branch wobbled, then slowly fell forward across the abyss – cra-a-asshh! – and the other end landed on the far side.

"A bridge!" shouted Stanley and Knots. "We've made a bridge."

Peckish hopped across it first

to show them how easy it was.
Stanley took more time. He
looked down into the abyss; it
was a long way to the bottom.
He took a deep breath. He sat
on the bridge with a leg either
side. He sl-o-wly edged across
until he reached the far side.

"Phew," he said. "That wasn't much fun."

Knots began to edge across the same way. But when he got to the middle, he stopped.

"I feel dizzy," he said.

"No you don't," said Stanley

firmly. "Come on, just a little further. Why don't you shut your eyes and think of your ship?"

"Ah, yes, my ship," replied Knots. He shut his eyes and edged a little further across while he thought of his ship.

"Now think of the seagulls,

and the sun shining on the sea,"
suggested Stanley.

"Ah, yes, the seagulls and the
sea," said Knots, and he edged
a little further over.

"Now think of the spray and
the sea breezes," said Stanley.

"Ah, yes," said Knots. He
held up his face to feel the spray
and sniff the breezes – and he
edged along a little more.

"*Got* you," said the little
explorer. He pulled his friend
on to firm ground.

"Phew," gasped Knots, mopping his face. "That's better. I don't mind having lots of water under me, but it's not much fun having lots of nothing!"

"You deserve a drop of beetroot wine," said Stanley.

He handed the bottle to Knots, who took a swig.

"Wow," he said. "That puts hairs on your chest."

After that they all had a little snooze.

7 Climbing the Cliffs

The next day they came to the end of the jungle. There were no more trees. But there in front of them was a wall of rock – they had reached the Cliffs of Pickapetal. Stanley and Knots stood with their heads back, staring up to the very top.

"We've got to get up there," said the little explorer.

"My eye," gulped Knots. "It's higher than any mast I've ever climbed."

"Are you good at climbing?" asked Stanley.

"Fair to middling," Knots replied.

"Then you must lead the way," said Stanley.

Knots gulped again.

"Aye, aye, cap'n," he said.

He spat on his hands and began to climb. First a foot, then a hand, then the other foot, then the other hand.

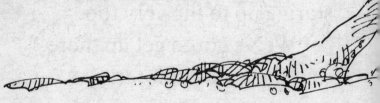

The little explorer followed, using the same footholds as Knots. Peckish was flying round and round beside them. If Stanley forgot where Knots had put his foot or his hand, Peckish showed him the way with her beak.

At last Knots got to the top
and stood up. Then he bent over
and pulled the little explorer up
beside him. They sat back and
admired the view.

"My eye," gasped Knots.

All they could see for miles and miles was the roof of the jungle. Only in the far distance was there a line of blue.

"Sea ahoy!" said Knots. He put his nose in the air to try and smell the sea breeze. Then he

glanced at his friend. Stanley
was looking very upset. "Hey,
what's the matter?"

"We're here," he said.
"We've come all this way, and
we've climbed to the top of the
Cliffs of Pickapetal. But *where*'s
the pinkafrillia?"

8 The Pinkafrillia at Last

They stared this way and that. All round them were huge rocks. There were no flowers anywhere – not even any grass. Stanley looked very sad.

"It must be here somewhere," he said.

He looked at his map. Knots stood up. It was very hot. He

shaded his eyes as sailors do
when they look out to sea but
he, too, could see only rocks.
Peckish peered at the map. She
pecked Stanley's helmet, tap-
tap-tap.

"Lee-eave it to me-ee!" she
screeched. "I'll find the
pinkafrillia."

She flew straight up in the air, then round and round in circles, looking down at the ground. Suddenly she disappeared from sight.

A few minutes later she shot back. Stanley stretched out his arm for her to land on. She looked very excited. She pulled at Stanley's coat, then flew off. They followed her. At last they came to a huge rock. It was split right down the middle, and growing in the crack was . . . the pinkafrillia.

"Wow," gasped the little explorer.

"Cor," said Knots the sailor.

They stared at the beautiful pinkafrillia, the only one in the world. It was shaped like a bell, about as big as your hand. The bell was striped all round with pink: the pink of candyfloss, the pink of strawberry ice-cream, the pink of rosy cheeks, the pink of flamingos and the pink of the sky at sunset. And all round the bottom of the bell were frills.

"Amazing . . ." said Stanley.

"Cor . . ." said Knots again.

They stared at the wonderful flower. Then they saw to their dismay that the frilly bell was beginning to droop.

"It's wilting," cried Stanley.

"It's too hot," said Knots,
mopping his face. "It needs
shade."

The little explorer pulled off his helmet and held it over the pinkafrillia to shade it from the sun.

"It's going to die," said Knots.

"No, no," cried Stanley, "it *must*n't die – it's the only one left in the world."

"It needs a drink," said
Knots.

"But there's no water round
here," said Stanley.

Peckish squawked at him
loudly.

"Of *course*," exclaimed
Stanley, "the beetroot wine.
There's a little left."

He grabbed the bottle and
poured the last drops of wine on
to the roots of the pinkafrillia.
They held their breath and
watched. In a few minutes the

flower sl-o-wly began to lift its
pink bell.

"Saved it – just in time," said
Stanley. "Good old Auntie
Annie."

Suddenly there was a funny sound, blip-blap-blop, and three fat pods dropped on to the ground under the pinkafrillia.

"Seed pods!" cried Stanley. "The pinkafrillia has given us each a seed pod. Oh, thank you, pinkafrillia."

"I'll plant mine here," said Knots.

"Yes, he-eere," agreed
Peckish.

They each dropped their seed
pods into cracks in the rock.

"I shall take my seed pod
home," said Stanley. "I shall
plant the seeds in my greenhouse.

Just fancy – pinkafrillias in my greenhouse!"

There was a sudden clap of thunder.

"Rain clouds on the way," said Knots. "There'll soon be plenty for the pinkafrillia to drink. Come on, cap'n, we'd better get going."

The little explorer gazed at the wonderful flower for the last time.

"Goodbye, pinkafrillia," he whispered. "I'm so glad we found you. And thank you for the seed pods. Goodbye . . ."

9 Home

They went back a different way. It was downhill through the jungle for six days and six nights. On the seventh morning they left the jungle behind them. In front of them lay the sparkling sea again.

"Cor," said Knots. "There's
not a sight like that in the
world."

He began to whistle, and
quite forgot the blisters on his
heels.

They made their way to the
harbour. And there was the
ship, waiting to pick them up.
Knots was the first to run up the
gangplank. He shook the
captain's hand.

"I'm back," he cried. "I've had enough of being an explorer – from now on it's a life at sea for me."

"Right," said the captain, "then make ready to cast off."

"Aye, aye, cap'n," said Knots.

He turned and helped the little explorer on board.

"Thanks for letting me be an explorer with you," said Knots. "But now I know it's a life at sea for me."

"Yes, I thought so," said Stanley. He looked at Peckish who was sitting on his arm, "And I suppose it's a life in the jungle for you, is it?" he asked sadly.

"Me-ee?" screeched Peckish. "No fee-ear! Don't le-eave me-ee he-eere!"

"You mean you'd like to stay with me? And come home and live with me and Auntie Annie?"

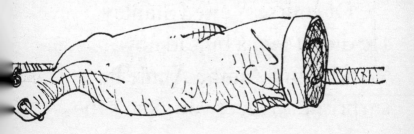

   "May I, ple-eease?"
squawked Peckish. She laid her
head on his shoulder, "Ple-
eease . . .?"
   "Of course," cried Stanley.
He didn't feel a bit sad now.
"And won't Auntie Annie be
surprised to meet you. She's the

one who makes the beetroot
wine, you know."

"Whee-ee-ee!" cried Peckish,
hopping up and down at the
thought.

"Cast off," called the captain.

"Aye, aye, cap'n," said
Knots.

The little explorer stood on deck with Peckish on his arm. The boat moved further and further away from the steaming jungle of Allegria.

"I think I've seen enough of the world – for now," said Stanley. "After all – east, west, but home's best."